A Note to Parents and Caregivers:

Read-it! Readers are for children who are just starting on the amazing road to reading. These beautiful books support both the acquisition of reading skills and the love of books.

The PURPLE LEVEL presents basic topics and objects using high frequency words and simple language patterns.

The RED LEVEL presents familiar topics using common words and repeating sentence patterns.

The BLUE LEVEL presents new ideas using a larger vocabulary and varied sentence structure.

The YELLOW LEVEL presents more challenging ideas, a broad vocabulary, and wide variety in sentence structure.

The GREEN LEVEL presents more complex ideas, an extended vocabulary range, and expanded language structures.

The ORANGE LEVEL presents a wide range of ideas and concepts using challenging vocabulary and complex language structures.

When sharing a book with your child, read in short stretches, pausing often to talk about the pictures. Have your child turn the pages and point to the pictures and familiar words. And be sure to reread favorite stories or parts of stories.

There is no right or wrong way to share books with children. Find time to read with your child, and pass on the legacy of literacy.

Adria F. Klein, Ph.D.
Professor Emeritus
California State University
San Bernardino, California

For Manuel and Camille, my two little dinosaurs, who sometimes wonder whether ...

First American edition published in 2005 by
Picture Window Books
5115 Excelsior Boulevard
Suite 232
Minneapolis, MN 55416
877-845-8392
www.picturewindowbooks.com

First published in Canada in 1999 by
Les éditions Héritage inc.
300 Arran Street, Saint Lambert
Quebec, Canada J4R 1K5

Printed in the United States of America.

Library of Congress Cataloging-in-Publication Data
St-Aubin, Bruno.
Daddy's a dinosaur / written and illustrated by Bruno St-Aubin.
p. cm. — (Read-it! readers)
Summary: A child describes a father who stomps around the house, swallows his breakfast in one gulp, and snores like a dinosaur, but may not be what he seems.
ISBN 1-4048-1028-5 (hardcover)
[1. Fathers—Fiction. 2. Dinosaurs—Fiction. 3. Family life—Fiction.] I. Title: Daddy is a dinosaur. II. Title. III. Series.

PZ7.S7743Dad 2004
[E]—dc22   2004023914

Daddy's a Dinosaur

Written and Illustrated by
Bruno St-Aubin

Special thanks to our advisers for their expertise:

Adria F. Klein, Ph.D.
Professor Emeritus, California State University
San Bernardino, California

Susan Kesselring, M.A.
Literacy Educator
Rosemount - Apple Valley - Eagan (Minnesota) School District

PiCTURE WiNDOW BOOKS
Minneapolis, Minnesota

Daddy works at home.

He's a little weird sometimes.

Mommy thinks he's too pale.

He gets strange looks from people.

At home, Daddy stomps around the house.

Mommy laughs at him, which gets him all steamed up.

At night, he takes all the sheets and blankets ...

10

and starts snoring like a dinosaur!

This morning, Daddy is really hungry.

He swallows his breakfast in a single gulp!

Then he takes me and my brother sledding.

It's so cool!

Afterward, Daddy looks at my homework.

But he isn't very helpful.

At bedtime, he tells me stories.

And I have bad dreams all night long!

Daddy likes to try to scare me.

I pretend I'm not afraid.

But my friends are!

And I can see why!

When Daddy cleans the house, he turns
everything upside down!

He has his own way of scrubbing the floors.

Meanwhile, Mommy goes to the grocery store.

When she comes back, she's in for a
big surprise.

Sometimes, Daddy cries.

When he does, we need our umbrellas.

In spite of everything, Daddy's very nice to us.

We love our dinosaur daddy! But is he
really a dinosaur?

More *Read-it!* Readers

Bright pictures and fun stories help you practice your reading skills. Look for more books at your level.

Alex and the Team Jersey by Gilles Tibo
Alex and Toolie by Gilles Tibo
Clever Cat by Karen Wallace
Daddy's a Busy Beaver by Bruno St-Aubin
Daddy's a Dinosaur by Bruno St-Aubin
Felicio's Incredible Invention by Mireille Villeneuve
Flora McQuack by Penny Dolan
Izzie's Idea by Jillian Powell
Mysteries for Felicio by Mireille Villeneuve
Naughty Nancy by Anne Cassidy
Parents Do the Weirdest Things! by Louise Tondreau-Levert
Peppy, Patch, and the Postman by Marisol Sarrazin
Peppy, Patch, and the Socks by Marisol Sarrazin
The Princess and the Frog by Margaret Nash
The Roly-Poly Rice Ball by Penny Dolan
Run! by Sue Ferraby
Sausages! by Anne Adeney
Stickers, Shells, and Snow Globes by Dana Meachen Rau
Theodore the Millipede by Carole Tremblay
The Truth About Hansel and Gretel by Karina Law
Willie the Whale by Joy Oades

Looking for a specific title or level? A complete list of *Read-it!* Readers is available on our Web site: *www.picturewindowbooks.com*